The Good Little Wolf

A.H. BENJAMIN

ILLUSTRATED BY SARAH ASPINALL

BLOOMSBURY EDUCATION
Bloomsbury Publishing Plc
50 Bedford Square, London, WC1B 3DP, UK

BLOOMSBURY, BLOOMSBURY EDUCATION and the Diana logo
are trademarks of Bloomsbury Publishing Plc

First published in Great Britain in 2010 by A & C Black, an imprint of Bloomsbury Publishing Plc
This edition published in Great Britain in 2020 by Bloomsbury Publishing Plc

Text copyright © A.H. Benjamin, 2010
Illustrations copyright © Sarah Aspinall, 2010

A.H. Benjamin and Sarah Aspinall have asserted their rights under the Copyright,
Designs and Patents Act, 1988, to be identified as Author and Illustrator of this work

A catalogue record for this book is available from the British Library

ISBN: PB: 978-1-4729-7073-2; ePDF: 978-1-4729-7070-1; ePub: 978-1-4729-7069-5;
enhanced ePub: 978-1-4729-7071-8

2 4 6 8 10 9 7 5 3 1

Printed and bound in China by Leo Paper Products, Heshan, Guangdong

All papers used by Bloomsbury Publishing Plc are natural, recyclable products from wood grown
in well-managed forests and other controlled sources.

To find out more about our authors and books visit www.bloomsbury.com

Chapter One

Once there were two wolves who lived in a cave in a big dark wood. They were called Big Wolf and Little Wolf.

Little Wolf loved hearing stories, so Big Wolf always told him one at bedtime. Most of them were about wolves.

"Dad?" asked Little Wolf one night.
"Are all wolves bad?"
"Of course not," replied Big Wolf.
"They are in books," said Little Wolf.

"Those are just stories," said Big Wolf.
"You must not believe what they say.
Now go to sleep, it's late." And he
kissed Little Wolf good night.

It was a long time before Little Wolf fell asleep. But when he did, he had exciting dreams. He was in lots of stories… and he was the hero of each one!

"I'm going to be good today," said Little Wolf, the next morning at breakfast.

"Very well," smiled Big Wolf. "Then off you go."

Little Wolf trotted out of the cave, and into the woods.

"I'll show everyone wolves can be good," he said to himself. "Then someone can write a story about me!" He liked that idea very much.

Chapter Two

Soon Little Wolf came to a clearing. There he saw an old lady, who was picking mushrooms. She had grey hair and she was wearing glasses.

"She's a grandma," thought Little Wolf. He had seen pictures of grandmas in storybooks.

Then Little Wolf saw something else. A snake was in the grass behind the old lady. And she hadn't seen it!

"I must do something," thought Little Wolf. "The grandma is in danger!" With two quick leaps, he pounced on the snake. He grabbed it in his jaws and fiercely shook it about.

The old lady jumped up with surprise.
"You **bad wolf**," she shrieked.
"Leave my walking stick alone!"

Little Wolf dropped the snake and ran off as fast as he could. He didn't stop running until he came to the edge of the woods.

"I tried to be good," he panted. "It's not fair. I'll never be a hero now."

Chapter Three

Not far away, Little Wolf came to a field. There he saw some white, woolly creatures. Nearby, a tall, thin man was sitting on a rock eating his lunch.

"Those are sheep," thought Little Wolf. "And that's a shepherd." He had seen pictures of sheep and shepherds in storybooks.

Just then, one of the sheep moved away
from the group.
"What a naughty sheep," thought
Little Wolf. "I'll soon sort it out." And
he was off in a flash.

A moment later, he was chasing the sheep round and round the field. It was terrified and so were the rest of the flock.

"Baa! Baa!" they bleated, running all over the place.

Little Wolf did not know which sheep
to chase. First he chased one...

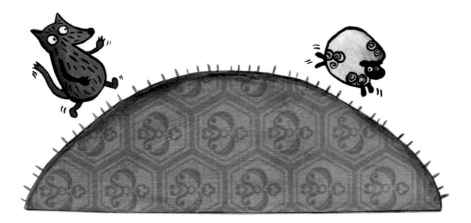

then he chased another.

The shepherd got to his feet and ran after Little Wolf with his long, crooked staff.

"You **bad wolf**," he shouted. "Leave my sheep alone!"

Little Wolf stopped chasing the sheep and fled. He didn't stop running until he came to a farm.

"I tried to be good," he panted. "*Twice*. But it's no use. I'll never be a hero now."

Chapter Four

Just then, Little Wolf noticed three pink animals with curly tails. They were shut in a dirty wooden pen.

"Those are pigs," thought Little Wolf. He had seen pictures of pigs in storybooks.

Little Wolf wondered why the pigs lived in such a horrible place. There was a nice cottage with a red door and blue windows not far away. Little Wolf was sure the pigs would prefer to live there instead.

"Maybe they haven't seen it," he
thought. "I'll show them where it is."
Little Wolf jumped inside the pen.

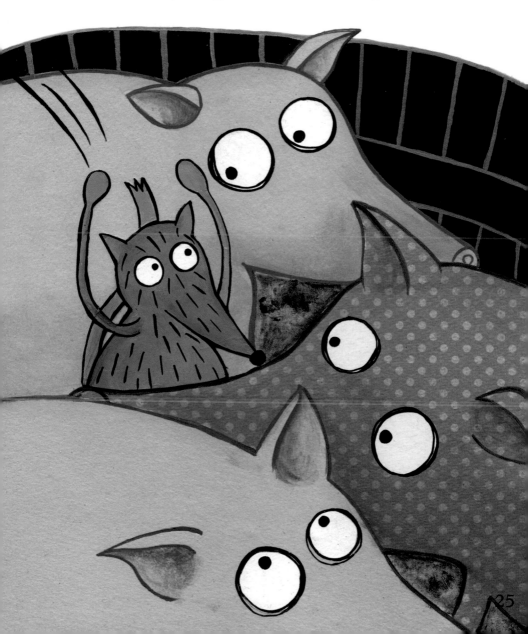

The pigs squealed with fright.
They broke down the fence and trotted
off down the lane.

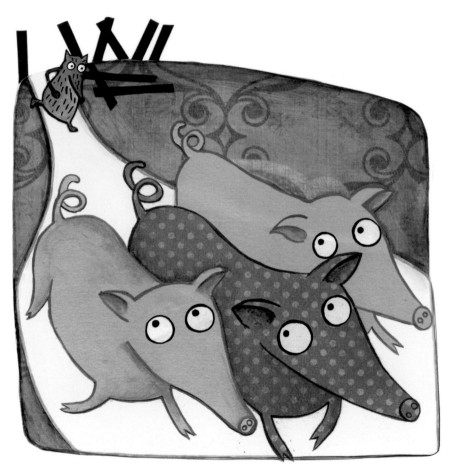

Little Wolf raced after them, leading
the pigs straight to the pretty cottage.

A young girl with a freckled face stuck her head out of the window. She looked very angry.

"You **bad wolf**," she screamed. "Leave my pigs alone!"

Little Wolf turned and scampered off.
He did not stop until he was back in
the woods again.

"I tried to be good," he panted. "*Three
times*. But it's not working. I'll never be
a hero now."

Chapter Five

Little Wolf was sad and fed up. He turned to go back home. He had not gone far when he saw a big, strong man chopping a tree with an axe.

"That's a woodcutter," thought Little Wolf. He had seen pictures of woodcutters in storybooks.

"They don't like wolves very much," thought Little Wolf. "I'd better keep away from him!"

He was just about to sneak off, when something happened.

The tree that the woodcutter was chopping suddenly started to fall. He had no time to get out of the way... and it landed right on top of him. **"Oh, no!"** gasped Little Wolf.

Luckily, the woodcutter was not hurt.
But he *was* stuck under the tree.
"Help! Help!" he shouted.

Slowly, Little Wolf came closer. He wanted to help. But how?

Just then, the woodcutter saw him. "A wolf," he cried. "That's all I need. Go away! Leave me alone!"

Little Wolf gave his face a friendly lick. Just to say, "I'm not going to hurt you."

"Oh," smiled the woodcutter. "Are you a good wolf? Will you help me?"

He handed Little Wolf his hat. "Here – take this to the village. When they see it, they'll know something's wrong. Please, my friend. Please hurry!"

Little Wolf took the hat in his mouth
and ran off as fast as he could.
"This is my chance to be a hero!" he
thought, with excitement.

Chapter Six

Soon Little Wolf reached the village.
The people spotted him at once.
"Wolf! Wolf!" they all shouted.

"That's a **bad wolf!**" croaked the old lady. "He tried to steal my walking stick!"

"He chased my sheep!" cried the tall, thin shepherd.

"He frightened my pigs!" squealed the girl with the freckled face.

"Oh, no!" sobbed a boy. "He's got my dad's hat in his mouth. He must have eaten him!"

"Come on," they shouted. "Let's get the **bad little wolf!**" Little Wolf turned on his heels and the whole village chased after him…

straight to the spot where the
woodcutter was trapped!

The villagers quickly moved the tree and the woodcutter got up gratefully. "Dad," cried the boy, hugging his father. "You're all right. We thought you had been eaten by the bad little wolf!"

"He's not a bad little wolf," said the woodcutter. "He's a **good little wolf**." Then he explained what had happened.
Everybody was amazed.

Little Wolf just stood there, looking very proud. He was a hero at last!

"Thank you!" said the little boy. "You saved my dad!"

Everyone cheered. "Hooray for the good little wolf!"

"I'm going to write a story about you," promised the woodcutter. "And I'm going to call it *The Good Little Wolf*."

Little Wolf smiled, as if to say, "I like the sound of that!" And happily, he trotted home.